CW00862755

LEILA

ليلـه

Because of Richard, who lives in my heart.
To Alexandre Jacques. G.L.

HAMISH HAMILTON CHILDREN'S BOOKS

Published by the Penguin Group
27 Wrights Lane, London W8 5TZ, England
Viking Penguin Inc., 40 West 23rd Street, New York, New York 10010, USA
Penguin Books Australia Ltd, Ringwood, Victoria, Australia
Penguin Books Canada Ltd, 2801 John Street, Markham, Ontario, Canada L3R 1B4
Penguin Books (NZ) Ltd, 182–190 Wairau Road, Auckland 10, New Zealand

Penguin Books Ltd, Registered Offices: Harmondsworth, Middlesex, England

Published by Pantheon Books, USA under the title *Nadia the Wilful*
Adapted from *Nadia the Wilful* by Sue Alexander

Text copyright © 1983 Sue Alexander
Illustration copyright © 1986 Éditions du Centurion, Paris.

British Library Cataloguing in Publication Data
Alexander, Sue
Leila.
I. Title
813'.54[J]   PZ7
ISBN 0-241-12265-1

Printed in Great Britain by Cambus Litho, East Kilbride

LEILA

Adapted from the story
by Sue Alexander
illustrated by Georges Lemoine

Hamish Hamilton · London

Leila was ten years old.
She was a child of the desert, where the
Bedouin travel on their camels through the
endless expanse of shifting dunes. Leila ran like
the wind. Her temper flashed like the swift
streams that flooded the dry river beds after a
storm. Among her people she was known as
Leila the Wilful.
Leila's father, Sheik Tariq, was a just man,
respected in all the desert encampments. But
even Tariq could not tame his headstrong
daughter Leila.

9

Leila had six brothers.
The oldest was Hamed. He was Sheik Tariq's
favourite son. Only he knew how to calm Leila
when she was in a rage. Only he could make
her laugh when she was gloomy and sad. Leila
and Hamed went everywhere together.

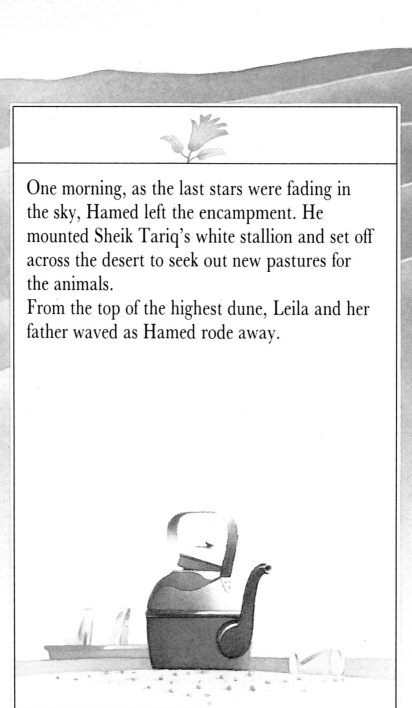

One morning, as the last stars were fading in the sky, Hamed left the encampment. He mounted Sheik Tariq's white stallion and set off across the desert to seek out new pastures for the animals.

From the top of the highest dune, Leila and her father waved as Hamed rode away.

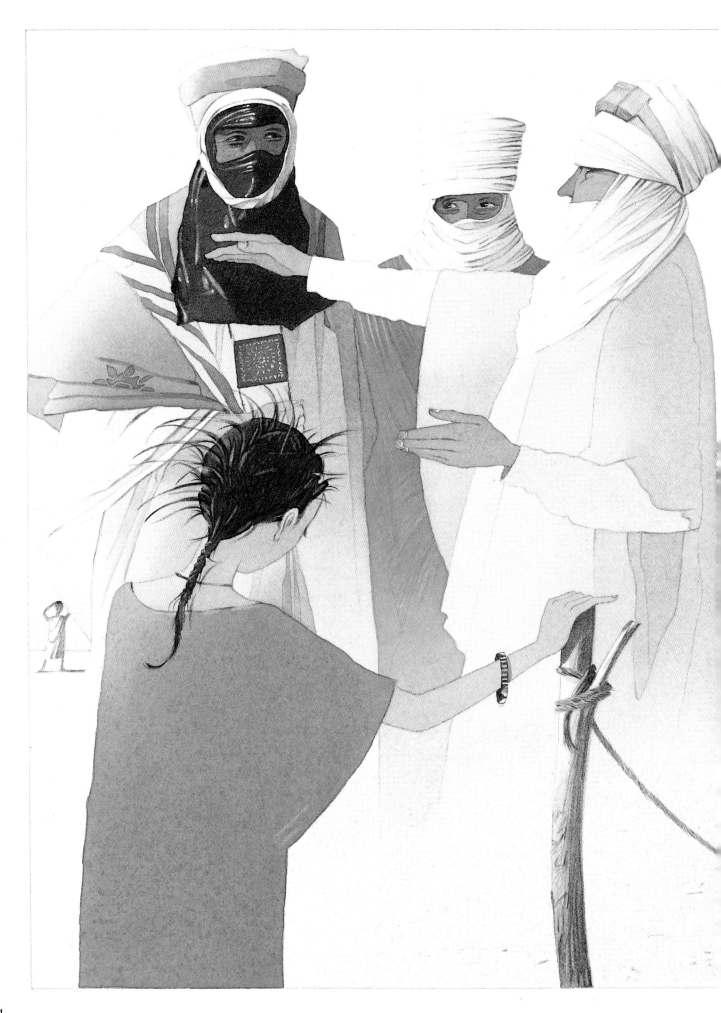

Day after day went by, but Hamed did not
return. Sheik Tariq set out to look for him,
travelling from one oasis to the next, asking
questions. Leila went with him.
A group of shepherds told them that they had
seen a white stallion, far away on the horizon.
But he carried no rider.
Passing merchants, their camels laden with
spices for the bazaar, talked of the emptiness of
the desert they had just travelled through. They
said to Tariq:
'Only Allah knows where your son is.'
Then Sheik Tariq understood that the sands
had taken his son, like so many Bedouin before
him.

When her father told Leila that she would never
see Hamed again, Leila screamed and fell,
beating the sand with her fists. No one could
take her brother away from her, not even Allah!
After a long time Tariq managed to calm her,
and they started the long journey back to their
encampment. As they travelled, Tariq fell
silent. When they reached home he went to his
tent and refused to eat anything, or to speak.
Leila wandered blindly through the oasis,
weeping.

After seven days, Tariq came out of his tent. He called his people together and said:
'From this day forward, anyone who speaks Hamed's name will be severely punished. I wish to forget what I have lost.'
Sheik Tariq's expression was hard and cold. The Bedouin bowed their heads. They were all uneasy, but no one dared to utter a word.

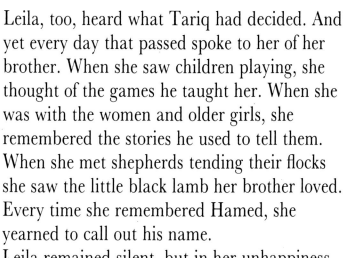

Leila, too, heard what Tariq had decided. And yet every day that passed spoke to her of her brother. When she saw children playing, she thought of the games he taught her. When she was with the women and older girls, she remembered the stories he used to tell them. When she met shepherds tending their flocks she saw the little black lamb her brother loved. Every time she remembered Hamed, she yearned to call out his name.

Leila remained silent, but in her unhappiness she wept and raged at anyone who crossed her path. Soon everyone in the oasis fled at the sight of her. Leila was lonelier than she had ever been before.

One day Leila saw her brothers playing a game
that Hamed had taught them. Without thinking
she said:

'That's not the way Hamed used to do it!'
Her brothers stopped playing and looked at
Leila with fear on their faces. She had broken
the silence. She was fortunate that Sheik Tariq
had not heard her.

Leila went into the women's tent. She began to
tell them of Hamed's stories. And she told how
he had made her laugh as he was telling them.
At first they were terrified and covered their
ears. Leila's mother said anxiously:
'Stop, Leila, what if your father should hear
you?'
But gradually the women began to listen. Soon
they were smiling at the stories, but Leila saw
her mother's worried look. She longed to make
her understand, but all she could say was:
'I have to talk about him, I have to!'
Then she ran away from the sound of her
mother's voice.

Leila went to find the shepherds up on top of
the dunes of sand. When they heard her utter
the forbidden name they moved away from her,
but she followed them. She told them how
Hamed used to love the little black lamb.
Slowly they gathered around her.
The more she talked about Hamed, the more he
seemed to be there, next to her. She could see
his smile and the light in his eyes. She could
hear his voice. Now she felt at peace. Soon
everyone was listening to her and smiling. It felt
as if Hamed were alive and sitting among them
again.

One evening, the youngest of the shepherds
came to the tent where Leila lived. He called to
her:
'Come and see how Hamed's little lamb has
grown!'
The tent opened, but it was Sheik Tariq who
came out. On his face was a look more fierce
than that of a desert hawk, and his words cut
like a sabre.

'Shepherd, it is forbidden for anyone to utter my son's name. You have disobeyed. You will leave this oasis and never return.'

Trembling, the shepherd went to gather his possessions.

The Bedouin lowered their eyes and were silent. They moved away from Leila and cast reproachful glances at her.

Leila longed to call out Hamed's name. She could feel the rage rising within her and choking her. She felt as if she were losing Hamed all over again.

Very early next morning Leila decided to go
and talk to her father, who sat alone, staring
out at the desert. Leila appeared suddenly
before him and in a quiet, faltering voice she
said:

'You will not steal my brother from me, I will
not let you!'

Tariq looked at her, his eyes colder than the
desert at dawn. Before he could speak she went
on:

'Can you see Hamed's face? Can you still hear
his voice?'

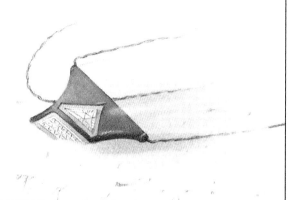

Tariq sat frozen with astonishment. Trembling, he answered:

'No, I cannot. Even though I gaze out into the desert for hours at a time.'

And his eyes filled with tears.

Gently, Leila said:

'Father, I know a way, listen . . .'

And she began to talk about Hamed. About how he used to walk with her, how he talked, played, told stories. How he knew the way to calm her, and to make her laugh when she was angry. She talked of happiness, tenderness and life . . .

Then she said:

'Now, Father, can you see his face again? Can you hear his voice?'

Tariq nodded and, for the first time in many weeks, he smiled.

'You see, Father,' Leila whispered, 'Hamed can still be with us.'

Tariq thought for a long time. Then he turned to Leila and said:
'Tell my people to gather here. I have something to say to them.'
When everyone had come together, Tariq said:
'My daughter Leila has given my beloved son Hamed back to me. Henceforth she will be known as Leila the Wise One. I want her name and that of Hamed to be honoured in all the desert encampments.'
A few days later the youngest shepherd returned to his flock, and kindness and happiness returned to the oasis.
And Hamed lived again in the hearts of all those who remembered him.